I went to t

ZOO

Written by
GRAHAM WILKINSON
Illustrated by Junis Laureano

Acknowledgement

I sincerely thank Bryony van der Merwe and her team for their skill and professionalism in helping me create this children's picture book. I could not have asked for anyone better, from editing, book design, proofreading and illustration to the final book files.

Also, to my beautiful partner Helen and our family for encouraging me to continue this project and giving me the confidence to believe in myself when I wasn't always sure whether I could do it. You are truly amazing.

Graham Wilkinson

First published in 2023

Written by Graham Wilkinson
Illustrated by Junis Laureano
Book design by Bryony van der Merwe

ISBN: 978-0-473-68549-2 (hardcover)
ISBN: 978-0-473-68548-5 (paperback)
ISBN: 978-0-473-68550-8 (ebook)

This book belongs to
and was a gift from

Aa

I went to the zoo. What did I see?

One angry alligator who said to me,

"Look at me. I'm quite a fright!

Watch your fingers. I might bite!"

1 one

Can you find more?

One active ant
One attractive apple
One anxious ape
One ancient acorn

Bb

I went to the zoo. What did I see?

Two brown bears who said to me,

"Please be quiet so we can sleep.

It's time for us to count our sheep!"

2 two

Can you find more?

Two busy bees
Two bossy baboons
Two brave beetles
Two bored badgers

Cc

I went to the zoo. What did I see?
Three cheeky chimps who said to me,
"We love swinging in the trees.
The zoo is the best place to be."

3 three

Can you find more?
Three charming cheetahs
Three clever camels
Three curious coyotes
Three cheerful chickens
? ? ?

Dd

I went to the zoo. What did I see?

Four docile donkeys who said to me,

"We are feeling bored today.

We need a new game to play."

4 four

Can you find more?

Four dapper ducks
Four daring dingos
Four devoted doves
Four dizzy dragonflies

Ee

I went to the zoo. What did I see?

Five enormous elephants who said to me,

"We are dirty, as you can see.

It's time for our bath at half past three."

5 five

Can you find more?

Five elegant emus
Five energetic elks
Five eager eagles
Five electric eels

I went to the zoo. What did I see?

Six frenzied frogs who said to me,

"Jump with us so high and free.

Like birds in the sky, we fly through the trees."

6 six

Can you find more?

Six friendly foxes
Six flying fireflies
Six feisty ferrets
Six flamboyant flamingoes

Gg

I went to the zoo. What did I see?
Seven graceful giraffes who said to me,
"We stand up straight. So grand and tall.
Eating leaves from trees, big, not small."

7 seven

Can you find more?

Seven groovy gorillas
Seven grinning geckos
Seven gleeful gazelles
Seven gentle gerbils

I went to the zoo. What did I see?

One zany zookeeper who said to me,

"It's six o'clock. It's time to go.

I'll be back tomorrow to put on a show!"

I went to the zoo. What did I see?

Two friendly faces who said to me,

"We've had a fun-filled day. That's plain to see.

It's time to go home. It's time for tea!"

ZOO

I went to the zoo. What did I see?

Three different animals looking at me.

A lion, a tiger, and a panda chewing bamboo.

The animals I saw when I went to the zoo.

About the author

I was born and educated in Huddersfield, West Yorkshire, England. I now live with my partner Helen and our family in the Scottish city of Dunedin in New Zealand. Most of my work has been spent in the manufacturing/ design industries. I am passionate about writing, especially picture books for children. Other interests include reading, drawing, travel, music and sport, especially cricket. I am an avid Arsenal football supporter.

Printed in Great Britain
by Amazon